Ladybird Readers

Frankenstein

Series Editor: Sorrel Pitts
Text adapted by Robert Hill
Illustrated by Monica Armino

LADYBIRD BOOKS

UK | USA | Canada | Ireland | Australia
India | New Zealand | South Africa

Ladybird Books is part of the Penguin Random House group of companies
whose addresses can be found at global.penguinrandomhouse.com.
www.penguin.co.uk   www.puffin.co.uk   www.ladybird.co.uk

First published 2018
001

Copyright © Ladybird Books Ltd, 2018

Printed in China

A CIP catalogue record for this book is available from the British Library

ISBN: 978-0-241-33615-1

All correspondence to
Ladybird Books
Penguin Random House Children's
80 Strand, London WC2R 0RL

MIX
Paper from
responsible sources
FSC® C018179

Frankenstein

To download full story audio in both British and American accents, and to complete the listening activities at the back of the book, visit www.ladybirdeducation.co.uk

Contents

Characters

Victor
Frankenstein

Frankenstein's
creature
(also called
"the monster")

Victor's father
and mother

Elizabeth

Justine

the family
in the cottage

CHAPTER ONE

The Arctic

My name is Victor Frankenstein, and I'm from Geneva in Switzerland.

A sailor called Captain Walton was exploring the **Arctic*** Sea, looking for a way to the **North Pole**. One night, he and his men found me lying on a broken **sled** on a large piece of ice in the sea. I was very thin and very tired.

"What are you doing here?" they asked me, as they helped me on to the ship.

"I'm following someone," I replied. "I must find him!"

*Definitions of words in **bold** can be found in the glossary on pages 63–64

"We saw an enormous man with dark hair walking on the ice last night," said Captain Walton.

When I was alone with Captain Walton, I told him my story.

———

I was very happy as a child. When I was five years old, my parents **adopted** a little girl called Elizabeth, who was my age. Some years later my parents had another boy, my brother, William.

When I was seventeen, I decided to study at a university in Germany with my best friend, Henry Clerval. Just when I was ready to leave, my mother suddenly became ill. Before she died she said, "Promise me you will marry Elizabeth!"

CHAPTER TWO

The Experiment

It was difficult to study at university, because I couldn't forget the death of my mother, and every day I felt so sad.

Then, I started going to **chemistry** lessons. The teacher talked about the wonderful things possible with modern science.

I started to ask myself, "Could I create life?"

I began collecting parts of dead bodies, and doing **experiments** in a small **laboratory** next to my bedroom. I was going to make a man!

I forgot my family, and worked hard for two years.

Then, one night in November, I was ready to start my experiment! I turned a wheel, and slowly, one eye opened. The creature started to breathe . . . but it was horrible!

He had yellow skin, and straight, black hair. I wanted to create something beautiful, but this was a monster!

I ran out of the laboratory, into my bedroom. I lay on the bed, but it was difficult to sleep, of course. When I finally slept, I had terrible dreams—I thought Elizabeth was dead!

Then, suddenly, I woke up, and saw something awful . . .

CHAPTER THREE
The Day After

The monster was standing in the door, looking at me. He was enormous—over two meters tall! His mouth opened and he made some sounds, but I couldn't understand them.

I was **terrified**, and ran downstairs. I walked around the streets all night, too frightened to return to my rooms.

In the morning, while I was walking around, I heard a voice which I knew.

"Victor! How are you?" It was my friend, Henry Clerval. "I've just returned from Geneva. Your father told me to look for you." He explained that my family were worried because I didn't write to them.

I went with Henry to my rooms, but I told him to wait downstairs—I was terrified that the monster was still upstairs. He wasn't there, but I **fainted** with fear and **exhaustion**. I was ill for months.

When I was better, I received a letter with some terrible news from my father. My little brother, William, was dead. He was found in the countryside, with **bruises** around his neck!

I hurried back to Geneva. Before going to my parents' house, I went to see the place where William's body was found.

When I arrived, there was an awful storm, and, in a **flash of lightning**, I saw something enormous in the trees. The monster was watching me!

CHAPTER FOUR

William and Justine

When I saw the monster, I ran away as fast as I could!

"He killed William," I thought, and I suddenly felt very afraid. I ran to my parents' house, and my father explained what happened.

"We were walking in the forest," he said. "William went to play, but he didn't return. We searched for him all night. In the morning we found him with bruises around his neck. He was dead.

"The police have **arrested** our dear Justine," my father continued. "She's worked for us since she was twelve years old! They discovered a **locket** in Justine's pocket. The locket belonged to William—it had a picture of his mother inside—but I can't believe Justine killed him!"

At the **trial**, Justine said that she, too, was looking for William that night. "I slept in a farm building for a few hours because I was tired," she said. "I can't explain why the locket was in my pocket."

I was sure that Justine was telling the truth, but I couldn't tell the **judge** about the monster. Elizabeth said good things about Justine, but the judge said she was guilty. She was **executed** the next day.

Chapter Five

Frankenstein Meets His Creature

I felt guilty for the deaths of William and Justine. They died because of my terrible experiment—because of my monster—but I couldn't say anything to anybody. "They will never believe my story!" I thought.

I became more ill, and my family persuaded me to rest in the mountains. One day, while I was walking, I saw something running quickly across the ice.

It was the monster!

"What do you want?" I shouted, angrily. "You've already killed my brother!"

"Everybody hates me, Frankenstein," he said. "I'm the unhappiest creature in the world. You created me, but you don't love me! Why?"

"I **regret** creating you!" I shouted. "Now, I only want to kill you!"

"I'm going to ask you something," the monster said. "If you promise to do it, I won't hurt your family. If not, I will kill you all! Now, follow me, and I shall tell you my story."

I followed the monster to a hut. We sat down by a fire, and he began to speak.

CHAPTER SIX

The Creature's First Months

"After I ran away from your laboratory, I hid in a forest," the creature said. "I ate nuts and fruit, and drank water from the rivers, but it wasn't enough. I needed more food.

"In a village, I saw vegetables in the gardens, and milk and bread on the tables in the **cottages**," he continued. "I liked it there, but when the people saw me, they screamed and threw stones at me."

The creature looked sad.

"Finally, I found an empty **hut**, and stayed there," he said. "It was near a cottage, where an old man lived with his son and daughter. They were poor, but they were good people.

"I used to hide outside the little house, and listen to them talking, laughing, and singing songs—that's how I learned to speak.

"One day, when the old man was alone, I went inside. I wanted to be his friend, and I brought him flowers. He was blind, so he wasn't frightened. He was kind to me, but, when his children came home and saw me, they called me a monster, and hit me with sticks."

CHAPTER SEVEN

Revenge

"I was still holding the flowers when I ran from the hut and hid in the forest," the creature continued. "I sat down by a lake, and saw my face in the water. I saw how ugly I was. Later, I went back to the cottage, but there was no one there. I was angry and sad, so I burned it.

"When I left your laboratory, I was wearing your coat. Your diary was in a pocket, and I taught myself to read. I read about your experiment, and how you made me! Then, I read that your home was in Geneva . . .

"I wanted **revenge!**

"In a forest outside Geneva, I found a boy. He screamed when he saw me. When I held him, he shouted, 'Let me go, you ugly monster! I'll call my father, Mr. Frankenstein!'

"I put my hands around the boy's neck, and he stopped shouting. Then, I saw a picture of a beautiful woman in a locket around his neck. Later, when I found a woman sleeping in a farm building, I put the locket in her clothes, so that she looked guilty. I have done some terrible things!

"I asked you to promise to do something, Frankenstein. Will you?"

CHAPTER EIGHT

The Creature's Wife

"I am sad and alone," said the creature. "Make me a wife! She must be as ugly as I am. Someone who won't be afraid of me. Someone who'll love me! If you do this, we'll go and live far away. You'll never see us again—I promise."

I agreed.

"Remember, I'll watch you all the time," said the monster.

Later, at home, my father asked, "Do you remember your promise to your mother, Victor? To marry Elizabeth?"

"Of course!" I said. Elizabeth was now a very beautiful woman, and I wanted to marry her, but I knew I had to make a female monster first.

I couldn't work at home, so I told my father I needed another holiday for my health. I went to Scotland with Henry Clerval. He stayed in a town on the coast, and I went to an island, where I started my terrible work.

I was worried all the time. "What will happen if these two monsters have children?" I thought.

One night, I saw the monster's face at the window, smiling! I couldn't continue, so I **tore** the body on the table into pieces.

The monster screamed, "You'll regret this. I'll see you on your wedding night!" Then, he ran away.

CHAPTER NINE
Henry Clerval

I was terrified by what the monster said.
I had to return to Elizabeth in Geneva.
She might be in danger!

I got into a boat, and sailed immediately to
the town on the coast where I left Henry.

When I arrived, I went immediately to
where Henry was staying. He was lying
on the bed, but he wasn't moving. I saw
bruises on his neck . . . he was dead!

I screamed.

When the police arrived, they found me
alone with the body. They arrested me.

I fainted with shock, and for days I couldn't speak. The police found letters from home in my pocket, and wrote to my father, who soon arrived.

At the trial, the judge said that there was no reason for me to kill Henry, and that he died before I arrived in his room—this proved that I was innocent.

My father took me home, and Elizabeth kissed me happily. Everyone was preparing for the **wedding**, but I remembered the monster's last words. I needed to be ready—I always carried a gun with me.

CHAPTER TEN

The Wedding Night

On our wedding day, I hid my worry and fear. I smiled at everyone, but I couldn't forget the monster's words.

That evening, I was too worried to stay with Elizabeth. I told her to go to bed, and I locked the door. I started checking every room in the house.

Suddenly, I heard Elizabeth screaming!

I ran to the bedroom, but I was too late! Elizabeth was lying dead on the bed. The bruises from the monster's hands were around her neck!

The monster was at the window. He pointed at Elizabeth's body and laughed!

I reached for my gun, but he was already running away.

Soon after this, my father died of shock. I was now completely alone. William, Justine, Henry, Elizabeth, and my father were all dead because of my terrible experiment.

Now, *I* wanted revenge! "I'll find the monster and kill him!" I promised myself.

Before starting my search, I went to the **cemetery** where William, Elizabeth, and my father were buried.

As I was kneeling, I heard the monster laugh. "Everyone you love is dead," he said. "Now, I am happy."

CHAPTER ELEVEN

The End

I followed the monster for months, across land and sea, but always going north. Sometimes, people gave me news of him.

One day, I saw a message on a tree from the monster: "Follow me to the North Pole, where the ice and cold will be terrible for you, but not for me."

———

"Yesterday I saw him," I told Captain Walton, "but the ice between us broke . . . and now I'm here, with you."

I felt weak as I finished my story. I was dying. My last words to Captain Walton were, "If he comes here, please kill him."

The next day, Captain Walton found the creature standing over Frankenstein's body, and speaking to it.

"Frankenstein, it's too late to ask you to forgive me," the creature said. "You hated me, but I hate myself more. I didn't want to kill anyone. I wanted to be good. I only became bad because people hated me and hurt me, but I won't kill any more people."

Then, he jumped down from the ship, and disappeared into the ice and snow.

Activities

The activities at the back of this book help you to practice the following skills:

✏️ Spelling and writing

📖 Reading

💬 Speaking

🎧 Listening

❓ Critical thinking

🏵️ Preparation for the Cambridge Young Learners exams

1 **Are sentences 1—5 *True* or *False*?**
If there is not enough information write,
***Doesn't say*. Write the answers in your**
notebook. 📖 ✏️

1 Captain Walton and his men thought
Frankenstein was dead when they saw him.

2 They helped an enormous man with dark
hair on to their ship.

3 Victor Frankenstein was from Geneva
in Switzerland.

4 When he was a child, Victor's parents
adopted two children.

2 **Read the definitions. Write the correct**
words in your notebook. 📖 ✏️

1 to look after another person's child   a . . .
like it is your own

2 the part of the world that is furthest   A . . .
north, where it is very cold

3 this is used to carry people and   s . . .
things on snow and ice

4 the place on Earth that is most north   N . . .

3 Complete the sentences using words from Chapter Two. Write the full sentences in your notebook.

1 It was difficult for Victor to study at university, because . . .

2 Things at university changed for Victor when . . .

3 Victor wanted to create life, so he . . .

4 Then, one night in November, Victor . . .

5 Victor wanted to create something beautiful, but . . .

4 Talk to a friend about the characters below.

Victor Frankenstein is from Geneva in Switzerland. He . . .

5 **Read the sentences. If a sentence is not correct, write the correct sentence in your notebook.** 📖 ✏️

1 When Victor woke up, the monster was looking at him.

2 The monster made some sounds that Victor could understand.

3 Victor was terrified of the monster, and tried to kill him.

4 Victor and Henry went to Victor's rooms, and the monster was there.

5 Victor learned that his brother, William, was married.

6 Victor went to Geneva, and he saw the monster there—she was watching him!

6 **Describe Frankenstein's monster in your own words in your notebook.** ✏️ ❓

He is very tall . . .

7 Listen to Chapter Four. Answer the questions in your notebook. 🎧*✏️

1 Why did Victor suddenly feel afraid?

2 Where were they walking when William disappeared?

3 Who did they find the next morning?

4 Who did the police arrest for killing William? Why?

8 You are Justine. Your friend is a policeman. Ask and answer the questions, using the words in the box. 💬

> can't explain   look for   tired
> sleep   farm building   twelve years old

1 How long have you worked for the Frankenstein family?

2 What were you doing on the night that William disappeared?

3 Where did you go, and where did you sleep that night?

4 Why did you have William's locket in your pocket?

 *To complete this activity, listen to track 5 of the audio download available at www.ladybirdeducation.co.uk

9 Match the two parts of the sentences. Write the full sentences in your notebook.

1 Victor felt guilty, because his monster killed

2 Victor became ill, and went

3 One day, Victor saw the monster, and

4 The monster wanted Victor

a William and Justine.

b to do something for him.

c to the mountains to rest.

d the monster spoke to him.

10 Write Chapter Five as a play script.

It is winter, and Victor Frankenstein is walking across the mountains. Suddenly, he sees the monster.

Frankenstein: What do you want?

11 Choose the correct words, and write the full sentences in your notebook.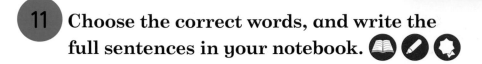

1 laboratory	university	forest
2 water	clothes	food
3 stones	bread	sticks
4 house	hut	village

1 At first, the monster hid in a . . .

2 But he needed more . . . , so he went to a village.

3 The people screamed and threw . . . at the monster.

4 The monster found an empty . . . near an old man's cottage.

12 Read the answers, and write the questions in your notebook.

1 An old man, with his son and daughter.

2 By listening to them talking and singing songs.

3 Because he was blind.

4 The old man's children.

13 **Choose the correct words, and write the full sentences in your notebook.** 📖 ✏️

1 The monster saw how **ugly / terrible** he was in the water.

2 The monster went back to the **forest, / cottage,** and burned it.

3 He used Victor's diary to learn how to **speak. / read.**

4 The monster found a **boy, / man,** and put his hands around his neck.

14 **Ask and answer the questions with a friend. Then, ask your own questions.** 💬

1 *Why did the boy scream when he saw the monster?*

Because he thought the monster was enormous and ugly.

2 Who was the boy?

3 Who did the monster find sleeping in a farm building?

4 What did the monster put in her pocket?

15 **Choose the correct answers, and write the full sentences in your notebook.**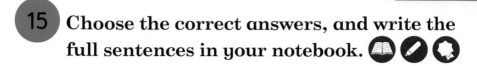

  1 What did Victor agree to make for the monster?

  a a wife   **b** a friend

  c a brother   **d** a mother

  2 Where did Victor go to start his work?

  a a cottage   **b** an island

  c a laboratory   **d** a university

  3 What was Victor worried the monsters might have?

  a children   **b** the locket

  c friends   **d** clothes

  4 Who did Victor see at the window?

  a Elizabeth   **b** William

  c his father   **d** the monster

  5 What did Victor tear to pieces?

  a the body   **b** the locket

  c a letter   **d** a cottage

16 **Listen to Chapter Eight. Describe the monster's plan in your notebook.**

First, the monster wanted Frankenstein to make him a wife . . .

*To complete this activity, listen to track 9 of the audio download available at **www.ladybirdeducation.co.uk**

17 Read the text, and write all the text with the correct verbs in your notebook. 📖 ✏️

Victor went to where Henry was staying and

. . . (**find**) him on the bed—he was dead! Victor

screamed, but when the police . . . (**arrive**)

they arrested him. The police . . . (**write**) to

Victor's father, and he . . . (**travel**) to Scotland

to help him. The judge . . . (**say**) that Victor was

innocent, so he . . . (**go**) home with his father.

18 Look at the picture and read the questions. Write the answers in your notebook. 📖 ✏️ ✳️

1 Where is Victor?

2 Who is happy to see Victor when he arrives at home?

3 What is everyone preparing for?

4 Why does Victor always carry a gun with him?

19 **Read the text. Find the five mistakes, and write the correct sentences in your notebook.** 📖 ✏️

On the evening of his wedding, Victor heard the monster scream. He ran to the bedroom, and he found Elizabeth lying on the floor—she was dead. The monster laughed as he walked away. Soon after this, Victor's brother died of shock, and then Victor wanted revenge. He decided to find the monster, and arrest him.

20 **Write the answers to the questions in your notebook.** 📖 ✏️ 💬

1 Why did Victor lock the bedroom door?

2 Why was Victor now completely alone?

3 Where did Victor go before he started his search?

4 What did Victor hear at the cemetery?

21 Who said this? Report the statements below in your notebook. 📖 ✏️

Victor   the creature

1 "Frankenstein, it's too late to ask you to forgive me."
The creature told Frankenstein that it was too late to ask him to forgive him.

2 "Please kill him."

3 "Sometimes, people gave me news of him."

4 "I won't kill any more people."

5 "I wanted to be good."

22 Read page 48. Write a different end to the story in your notebook. ✏️ ❓

The next day, Captain Walton saw the creature . . .

Project

23 **Write a review of this book in your notebook. Did you like it? Why? / Why not?**

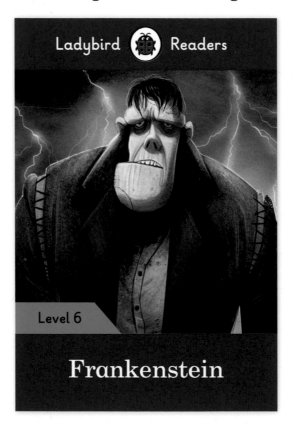

Ladybird 🐞 Readers

Level 6

Frankenstein

In your review, include the following information:

- which character you like the most

- what part of the story you like the most

- which picture you like the most

Glossary

adopt *(verb)*
to look after another person's child like it is your own

Arctic *(noun)*
the part of the world furthest north, where it is very cold

arrest *(verb)*
when police take a person to a police station and keep them there, because the police believe they have done something wrong

bruise *(noun)*
a dark mark that appears under the skin when someone falls or is hit

cemetery *(noun)*
a place where dead people are put in the ground

chemistry *(noun)*
a kind of science

cottage *(noun)*
a small house

execute *(verb)*
to kill a criminal because a judge has ordered it

exhaustion *(noun)*
When you are very, very tired you are exhausted. *Exhaustion* is the noun of exhausted.

experiment *(noun)*
a test done in science to find out new information

faint *(verb)*
to fall down suddenly and not be awake

flash of lightning *(noun)* During a storm, a *flash of lightning* might appear in the sky.

hut *(noun)*
a very small building, often made from wood

judge *(noun)*
A person in a court, whose job is to decide if a person has broken the law. A *judge* decides what happens to a criminal.

laboratory *(noun)*
a room where science experiments are done

locket *(noun)*
a necklace with a person's picture in it

North Pole *(noun)*
the place on Earth that is most north—it is in the Arctic

regret *(verb)*
to feel sorry about something you have done, and to wish you had done something differently

revenge *(noun)*
something bad you do to someone, because they have done something bad to you

sled *(noun)*
this is used to carry people and things on snow and ice

tear (past simple: tore) *(verb)* to pull, or cut, something into pieces

terrified *(adjective)*
very, very frightened

trial *(noun)*
a meeting in a court, where a judge decides if a person has broken the law

wedding *(noun)*
a special day, often in a church, where two people get married